DRIP!

Written by: Jan Butler
Illustrations by: Raynald Kudemus

A. The book targets rooms of the house, categorization/association activities with objects that belong in particular rooms, a mysterious noise, synonymous words for "drip", a humorous twist with technology verses Grammy and Grampy, problem solving, predicting, and an "I- spy" activity within the illustrations. The text plays with words – fun sounding words, rhyming words, and made up words. The text is repetitive, rhymed and melodic making it easy to follow the rhythm and fluency of speech. The rhyming pairs and synonymous words provide vocabulary expansion opportunities for young readers.

B. Ages 4 – 8, Grades K – 3. Theme – Fiction, Mysterious Noise, Grammy/Grampy, rooms of the house, stories in rhyme, technology.

To order additional copies of this book, contact:
Xlibris Corporation
1-888-795-4274
www.Xlibris.com
Orders@Xlibris.com

This story has been inspired and dedicated to my husband, Steve, the "Drip Detective." I would like to thank one of the most inspiring children's literacy instructors at the University of Southern Maine, Mrs. Susan Dee, for her encouragement, guidance, and support.

**Grammy bent down to feed her cat, Nip
When all of a sudden she heard. . .**

drip!

Drip!

DRIP!

She yelled, "Grampy come HERE!
Something is in this room!"
Grampy came running waving the garage broom.

Swinging it fast! Swish! Swoosh! Swish! Swoosh!
With hands on her hips Grammy shouted,
"Shoosh! Grampy, SHOOSH!"

Grampy stood silent, hanging his lip,
His ears grew **bigger** as he heard

**Run to the kitchen, to the sink take a peek,
Maybe under the fridge there is a trickling leak.**

Not over here! Not over there!
They can't find that drip anywhere
drip! Drip! DRIP!

In the bathroom pipes the dribble must be
"I'll look in the tub!" "I'll check out the TV!"

Not over here! Not over there!
They can't find that drip anywhere

drip!

Drip!

DRIP!

Hang out the attic window!   Look on the roof!
Seeping down the wall, that will be the proof.

Not over here! Not over there!
They can't find that drip anywhere

drip!

Drip!

DRIP!

The **BASEMENT!** That's the place it must be,
The furnace is oozing, just wait and see.

Not over here! Not over there!
They can't find that drip anywhere

drip!

Drip!

DRIP!

Not over here! Not over there!
They can't find that drip anywhere

drip!

Drip!

DRIP!

**Run to the dining room. Look on the floor.
It could be the heater. It has leaked before.**

Not over here! Not over there!
They can't find that drip anywhere

drip!

Drip!

DRIP!

To the fish tank in the living room, I know that I'm right!
Nip loves to watch and play with the Beta fish at night.

Not over here! Not over there!
They can't find that drip anywhere

drip! Drip! DRIP!

**Leaning down low and raising his brow,
Grampy said, "Grammy, you are dripping somehow!"**

Both stood there listening
To the dripping sound,

First they looked up

And then to the ground

"The sound is your pocket,
That's where it's at!"

"Nnnnnnooooo!" whispered Grammy,
It must be the cat."

Grammy reached into her pocket
And pulled out her iPhone.
The drip was her new game
'Poodle Jump,' fetching his bone.

Grampy stared at Grammy with a grin on his face,
He was the dribble detective who solved this leaky case.

"Come, Grampy, SIT! And play for a while.
Let's make poodle jump for more than a mile."

**Grammy held the phone as the two sat down,
But both fell asleep from running aroun'.**

LEARNING ACTIVITIES

1. **I Spy:** An iPhone is hidden in each illustration. Use the "I Spy" activity to evoke descriptive language and basic concept words. Rather than simply pointing at the hidden iPhones, encourage young readers to describe where the iPhones are hidden on each page (*i.e. I see the iPhone on the **right** side of the page **near** the **top** and it **looks like** a shelf / I see the iPhone on the **left** page, **under** Nip's food and it's **shaped like a rectangle**, it is Nip's placemat*).

2. **Vocabulary/Language Expansion Activities:**

   SYNONYMS   Find the synonymous words for drip (*trickling, leak, dribble, seeping, oozing*). Use colorful language by brainstorming other words within the text that could replace a word, yet keep its meaning (*i.e. <u>Run</u> to the kitchen – jog, scamper, sprint, dart, scurry, rush, hurry / <u>Hang</u> out the attic window – suspend, dangle, droop*).

   CATEGORIZATION / ASSOCIATION. Target rooms of the house. Categorize and associate objects found in various rooms (*i.e. living room: couch, TV, chairs, end tables, floor lamp, etc.*). Have the children design a home with various rooms and floors and decorate/furnish their homes.

3. **Phonological Awareness Activities:** After reading the story aloud several times, use the following activities to help develop phonological awareness skills. Activities can be completed with a whole group, small group, or individually (***NOTE: These activities should not be used with print because the skills that are targeted are auditory skills***). Begin at the level appropriate for your child.

   RHYMING (***Definition: When the middle and the end of the words sound the same, the words rhyme***). Find the rhyming pairs within the story (***Nip/drip, room/broom, swoosh/shoosh, lip/drip, peek/leak, there/anywhere, be/TV, roof/ proof, be/see, bed/head, floor/before, right/night, brow/somehow, sound/ground, at/cat, phone/bone, face/case, while/ mile, down/aroun'***). Rhyme Discrimination: Do these words rhyme? <u>Nip – drip</u> {*yes*}; <u>peek – bed</u> {*no*}. Rhyme Production: Tell me a word that rhymes with <u>room.</u> Rhyming game – I am thinking of something in the dining room that rhymes with cable...(***table***), that rhymes with wish...(***dish***), that rhymes with late...(***plate***), etc. Target vocabulary in all the rooms.

   SYLLABLE SEGMENTATION (Arm tapping, use manipulatives, make dashes, make bones and poodle jump). Say a word and then child taps and says syllables. Each bone represents a syllable (*i.e. Grammy / Gram–my; anywhere / an–y– where; bedroom / bed-room*). Brain storm items found in rooms of the house and tap out syllables (*i.e. kitchen / kit-chen; microwave / mi-cro-wave*).

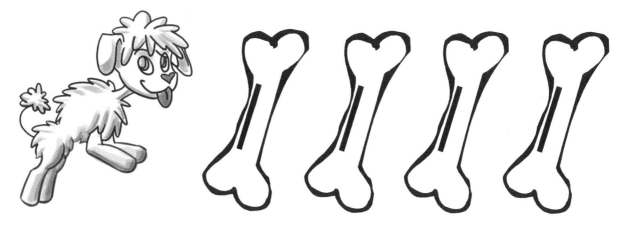

CPSIA information can be obtained
at www.ICGtesting.com
Printed in the USA
LVHW071413130520
655518LV00014B/1083